Dear Parents:

Congratulations! Your child is taking the first steps on an exciting journey. The destination? Independent reading!

STEP INTO READING® will help your child get there. The program offers five steps to reading success. Each step includes fun stories and colorful art or photographs. In addition to original fiction and books with favorite characters, there are Step into Reading Non-Fiction Readers, Phonics Readers and Boxed Sets, Sticker Readers, and Comic Readers—a complete literacy program with something to interest every child.

Learning to Read, Step by Step!

Ready to Read Preschool–Kindergarten
• big type and easy words • rhyme and rhythm • picture clues
For children who know the alphabet and are eager to begin reading.

Reading with Help Preschool–Grade 1
• basic vocabulary • short sentences • simple stories
For children who recognize familiar words and sound out new words with help.

Reading on Your Own Grades 1–3
• engaging characters • easy-to-follow plots • popular topics
For children who are ready to read on their own.

Reading Paragraphs Grades 2–3
• challenging vocabulary • short paragraphs • exciting stories
For newly independent readers who read simple sentences with confidence.

Ready for Chapters Grades 2–4
• chapters • longer paragraphs • full-color art
For children who want to take the plunge into chapter books but still like colorful pictures.

STEP INTO READING® is designed to give every child a successful reading experience. The grade levels are only guides; children will progress through the steps at their own speed, developing confidence in their reading. The F&P Text Level on the back cover serves as another tool to help you choose the right book for your child.

Remember, a lifetime love of reading starts with a single step!

For Lillian Freeman and her dog, Floyd
—I.C.

For Lorelei, always
—J.K.

Visit us on the Web!
StepIntoReading.com
randomhouse.com/kids

Educators and librarians, for a variety of teaching tools, visit us at
RHTeachersLibrarians.com

Library of Congress Cataloging-in-Publication Data
Cooper, Ilene.
Little Lucy goes to school / by Ilene Cooper ; illustrated by John Kanzler.
    pages cm. — (Step into reading. Step 3)
Summary: When Mom and Lucy the beagle go to school to deliver Bobby's forgotten lunch,
Lucy gets loose.
ISBN 978-0-385-36994-7 (pbk.) — ISBN 978-0-375-97179-2 (lib. bdg.) —
ISBN 978-0-375-98164-7 (ebook)
[1. Beagle (Dog breed)—Fiction. 2. Dogs—Fiction. 3. Schools—Fiction.] I. Kanzler, John, illustrator.
II. Title.
PZ7.C7856 Li 2014 [E]—dc23 2013024344

Printed in the United States of America

10 9 8 7 6 5 4 3 2 1

This book has been officially leveled by using the F&P Text Level Gradient™ Leveling System.

Little Lucy Goes to School

by Ilene Cooper
illustrated by John Kanzler

Random House 🏫 New York

Lucy was a little beagle.

She liked to run.

She liked to bark.

She liked to howl.

HOOOWL!

Most of all, she liked her boy,
Bobby Quinn.
And he liked her just as much!

Mornings were busy
at the Quinn house.
Mrs. Quinn made breakfast.
Mr. Quinn made the lunches.
Bobby ran around,
looking for his books.
Lucy just ran around.
After breakfast,
Mr. Quinn went to work.

Then it was Bobby's turn to leave.

He shook Lucy's paw.

"I have to go to school," he said.

"School is where I learn new things.

Be good, Lucy!"

Lucy flopped on the floor.

Things were quiet

when Bobby was gone.

Why couldn't Bobby stay home

and play?

Mrs. Quinn spotted something.

"Oh no!" she said.

"Bobby forgot his lunch."

Lucy looked up at Mrs. Quinn.

"Well, Lucy," she said,

"we will have to bring it to him."

Mrs. Quinn grabbed Bobby's lunch box.

She picked up Lucy.

Out they went.

The ride to the school was short.

Mrs. Quinn parked the car.

"I should have brought your leash,"

Mrs. Quinn told Lucy.

She picked up the lunch.

She picked up Lucy.

They hurried into the school.

Lucy looked around.

What was this new place all about?

Colored drawings hung on the wall.

A group of kids walked

through the hall.

This looked interesting!

Mrs. Quinn went into the school office.

A young woman stood by a desk.

"I'm Jill," she said.

"Can I help you?"

"Hi, Jill," Mrs. Quinn said.

"I'm Bobby Quinn's mother.

He forgot his lunch."

She held up the lunch box.

"I'll get it to him," Jill said.

"And who is this?"

She patted Lucy's head.

"This is Lucy," Mrs. Quinn said.

"Can I hold her?" Jill asked.

Mrs. Quinn started to hand Lucy over.

But before Jill could take her,

Lucy wiggled.

Then Lucy wriggled.

In a flash, she was free.

And when she was free,
she ran out the office door!
"Lucy!" Mrs. Quinn called.
Lucy heard her.

But she didn't stop.

There was too much to see

in this new place!

Lucy ran down a long hall.

She ran past a boy with brown hair

and a girl with a ponytail.

"It's a dog!" the boy said.

"Stop!" the girl called.

"Dogs don't belong in school!"

Lucy heard her,

but she didn't stop.

She followed her nose.

And her nose smelled food.

She scooted into a bright, shiny room.

Pots and pans sat on a big stove.

The good smells tickled her nose.

A woman in an apron

held a tray of sandwiches.

Lucy ran in circles
around the lady's legs.
She barked a little bark.
"Oh!" the lady said.
"What is a dog doing in this kitchen?"
A few sandwiches fell on the floor.

That was good news for Lucy.
She leaped on the sandwiches
and took some bites.
"Stop, little one," the lady said.
"Dogs don't belong in school."

She tried to grab a sandwich
from Lucy.

Then she tried to grab Lucy.

But Lucy was too fast.

She ran out the lunchroom door.

Now where?

Lucy followed her nose again.

A funny smell came from a room

with lots of books.

Lucy peeked in.

A man with a mop
was cleaning the floor.
Quietly, Lucy padded in.
She sniffed the floor.

The floor was wet.

Lucy's paws got wet.

She slid a little.

The man turned around.

He saw Lucy.

"Am I seeing things?" he asked.

Lucy barked.

He was not seeing things.

"Come with me, doggie,"

the man said.

"Dogs don't belong in the library!"

He made a move toward Lucy.

Lucy did not want to come
with the man.

Out of the library she ran.

She glanced behind her.

The man with the mop was after her.

So was the lady in the apron.

Mrs. Quinn came around the corner.

"Lucy, stop!" Mrs. Quinn called.

Lucy heard her,
but she didn't stop.
This was too much fun!

Lucy was fast.

No one could catch her.

She dashed down a hallway.

She saw an open door.

She scooted inside.

The room was full of children.

Lucy looked at them.

They looked back at Lucy.

Then she heard a voice she knew.

"Lucy!" Bobby called.

"What are you doing here?"

Bobby!

Lucy was so glad to see her boy.

She jumped into his lap.

She licked his face.

The kids left their seats.

They crowded around Bobby.

They had never seen a dog

in school!

Mrs. Lee, Bobby's teacher,
clapped her hands.
"Back to your seats, please," she said.
"Bobby, what is Lucy doing here?"

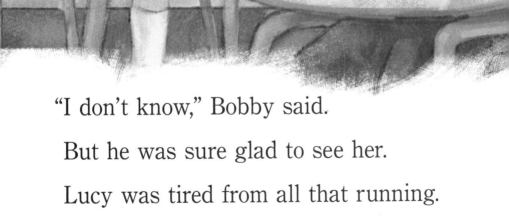

"I don't know," Bobby said.

But he was sure glad to see her.

Lucy was tired from all that running.

She curled up in Bobby's arms.

Just then the man with the mop,

the lady in the apron,

and Mrs. Quinn rushed into the room.

"There she is!" Mrs. Quinn said.

She pointed to Lucy.

"I brought Bobby's lunch to the office,"

she told Mrs. Lee.

"But Lucy got away!"

"It's all right," Mrs. Lee said.

"It's funny to have a dog in school—
at least for a little while."

Mrs. Quinn took Lucy from Bobby.

"It's time to go home," she said firmly.

"Dogs don't belong in school!"

Lucy yawned.

Maybe it was time to leave.

But she had learned a lot in school.

Sandwiches tasted good!

Wet floors were slick!

Running through halls was fun!

Bobby gave Lucy one last hug.

"I'll be home soon, Lucy," he said.

"We'll have more fun then."

Lucy licked Bobby's face.

Fun!

She could hardly wait.